SHACKLED TO CREATION

ALSO BY AVTAR SIMRIT

True Fiction (Volume One)
A Dream of True Time

Break Every Chain

SHACKLED TO CREATION

A Collection of Poetry

AVTAR SIMRIT

Apocalyptic Rhymes

For my dad;
like all things transform and grow,
we have both transformed so much since
these poems were first written.

I no longer need the Sealing Wax.
I love you.

Contents

PART FOUR
HOPEFUL DESPAIR

PART FIVE
WHAT THE BLIND SHALL SEE

PART SIX
TEAR OUT YOUR EYES AND I SHALL GIVE
YOU WISDOM

PART SEVEN
BECOMING EVERYTHING

Eleven Years Later

As the band Tears for Fears so aptly stated, "Funny how time flies." Sometimes it really does, doesn't it? It boggles my mind that it's already been eleven years since I originally published this collection of poetry. That's one year longer than a decade! *Shackled to Creation* is a decade old! And the years have seasoned it like a fine wine. To me, these poems still have as much zest, punch, and dark fun as they did when I first wrote them. In some moments of high lyricism, I even think they contain more flavor and are even more poignant today than they ever were. That being said, what is fascinating to me, from a psychological perspective, is that even though I still get so much enjoyment out of these pieces, and I feel them deep into my essence and my balls, I don't have any emotional connection to them anymore. I feel the pain from some of these pieces now as *empathy*, not as if the pain was my own and still fresh.

If you have read the second book in this duology of poetry collections, *Break Every Chain*, you will have been able to see the arc of spiritual and emotional transformation which was my journey through the years. That was my intention, yes; I'm always working in concepts. This is why I intentionally divide each book into seven parts with titles that sum up the theme of that step in the journey. Whenever I create a book, or a music album, it is on concept. So the way that that art is meant to be absorbed is from beginning to end, straight through. That is how I designed it and that is how it is intended to be taken in by the reader, or listener. Unfortunately, what I've come to realize—especially with collections of poetry and music albums—the reader or listener tends to 'jump around' to different poems or tracks on the album. Hence, a good portion of the meaning and story arc is lost that way if it's not taken in the way it was meant to be.

I am telling you now, dear reader, that this is how this collection and the one which follows—*Break Every Chain*—is meant to be read. Reading each part in order, each poem in sequence, the character arc and transformation will reveal itself to you; otherwise the meaning just gets muddled in the mayhem. For *Shackled to Creation*, I collected all of the poems I wrote in high school and college. This is important to note in order to put these pieces into context of when they were written: mostly from the consciousness of a wounded teenager trying to heal through the only way that worked for him—writing. In the introduction of *Break Every Chain*, I wrote about Shadow Work and using art to dive deep into your Shadow, integrate it, and transform. This is what I'm referring to here (reference the introduction in *Break Every Chain* for more info).

Parts one through four collect all the poems I wrote in high school. This segment makes up more than half of the book; that is from ages fourteen to eighteen. Then parts five through seven were written in the two years I was attending Film School. In these parts you can see the seeds of transformation that later sprout in the poems of *Break Every Chain*. Like I said before, everything is on concept. And when I was putting the poems together for this first volume, I already had a vision projected into the future of the second volume which would be the companion piece and culmination of all that had been planted in *Shackled to Creation*. From bondage to freedom and I would track the whole metamorphosis in two collections of verse.

In 2011, I was twenty-one years old, living in Providence, Rhode

Island, and decided it was finally time to publish *Shackled to Creation*. It pleases me greatly that I can now have this introduction to the new 11th Anniversary Edition where I can explain the context and ages I was when these poems were written. When it was originally published, there was no indication made as to when the pieces were written. For all the reader knew, they could all have been written in 2010 and then published the year after—which would have created a whole different precedent around the work. Now, hopefully this information will clear up any confusion or questions readers have as to whether the author still clings to the emotions heretofore expressed in these pieces.

Publishing was a foreign land to me at the time, and we learn from the mistakes we make—hopefully. I will not name here the vanity publisher which I used to originally publish the collection. If you wish to dig deep enough—probably not that deep—you can find it if you're curious; and know I'm not the only unsatisfied customer. There were a few things about that edition which weren't aligned with the vision I had for the book. For one, they totally threw out my cover design, and I wasn't inclined to fight them on it or pay more money than I already was. The whole project cost me a thousand dollars for a book that didn't even look the way I wanted it to. It pleases me immensely that now this edition has the cover design I meant for it; with the talented Monique Rebelle who created the full cover art from my rudimentary sketch that I did eleven years ago. Also the publishers squashed way too many words onto each page—which is cheaper print costs for them, but doesn't make for as pleasant a reading experience as I wanted. From the somewhat ugly-looking 130 pages, it has expanded out to over 200, and the formatting is to my liking.

My twenty-one year old self would have smacked me eleven years later to know that what I payed a thousand dollars for back then didn't get me the look of the book I wanted, and that today I would only have to spend fifty bucks to put it into the formatting and form I originally intended. What we learn throughout time really makes for a lot of face-palms.

To wrap this up into a complete infinity symbol; a genuinely sexy self-sucking ouroboros; I will connect the context of *Break Every Chain*, and then wrap it back around into a Silent Mobius strip. The Bootstrap Paradox making its debut in the circus of life—in the Clown World of the Mind. But I digress... *Shackled to Creation* is about ten years worth of poetry. And *Break Every Chain* is also about ten years worth of poetry. That is *two fucking decades* worth of verse—and you know me, I'm always ready to add a verse. When I came back to Chicago from Providence, I was twenty-two years old, and I started writing more poetry, knowing that it was all going to be collected in volume two. And that volume was finally published in the fall of the year 2021; I was about to turn thirty-two. An infinite amount of transformation happened in those ten years, and if you've read it, you know. While those poems were being written, I traveled to the West Coast, lived in a van while driving up through California, Oregon, and Washington. Then when I came back down to Southern California, that was when Kundalini Yoga found me—and the rest is past lives, future lives, and all incarnations expressing themselves simultaneously. In part six of *Break Every Chain*, you definitely will see where it takes that turn. I finished up the last few poems in Reno, Nevada. And as they say, "the rest is history."

But truly, in reality, it's not. There is no history. As Henry Ford once said: *"History is more or less bunk. It's tradition. We don't want tradition. We want to live in the present and the only history worth a tinker's dam is the history we make today."* And that's it! The only history worth a flying fuck is the history me make today, in the Present. In the Power of Now. There is no his-story, because there is no story—there is no *he*. There is no *me* and *you*. Because we are not separate. You are me and I am you. And there is no me. Identity is a fallacy, an illusion, a crockery. *Identity equals propaganda.* These poems were just as much written by you as they were by me. *We are everything and we are nothing.* These poems are just a mirror of what you already know to be true.

But then again, maybe they won't be. ;-)

I Love you so much!

—Avtar Simrit
Reno, Nevada
January 18, 2022

"Existence is an organic unity. It does not exclude anything; it is all-inclusive."
  - OSHO

"Art should comfort the disturbed and disturb the comfortable."
  - Cesar A. Cruz

"We don't have a great war in our generation, or a great depression, but we do, we have a great war of the spirit. We have a great revolution against the culture. The great depression is our lives. We have a spiritual depression. We have to show these men and women freedom by enslaving them, and show them courage by frightening them."
  - Chuck Palahniuk, *Fight Club*

We would rather be ruined than changed
We would rather die in our dread
Than climb the cross of the moment
And let our illusions die.
  - W.H. Auden

"I am a man, and men are animals who tell stories.
This is a gift from God, who spoke our species into being,
but left the end of our story untold.
That mystery is troubling to us. How could it be otherwise?
Without the final part, we think, how are we to make sense
of all that went before: which is to say, our lives? So we make
stories of our own, in fevered and envious imitation of our Maker,
hoping that we'll tell, by chance, what God left untold.
And finishing our tale,
come to understand why we were born."

- Clive Barker, *Sacrament*

PART ONE

A Farewell to Inspired Simplicity

Home in the City

Haven for Madness,
Bank of Negative Energy,
Stagnant Swamp of Willfully discarded memories,
Bottle for Built Up Anger,
A Divided Household,
House of Mixed Emotions:

I have been told that it is where all things were resolved and brought to the better end.

Yes, what happened there needed to happen.

I have been told that what could make us all truly happy was realized while in that house.

This is true; during this time there was the enlightenment of the true path to be taken.

And they say that it is where I learned to stand on my own.

I say yes, I did learn to think for myself.

And I have agreed with you on these, but I was there and I know exactly how

Overwhelmingly evil it was:

Tell me why it is healthy to live in a house that is a hotel for lies and the demons of

Falsehood.

Five years the air in there became thick and heavy with the
screams and suppressed
       Emotions of turmoil and mental violence;

Depressing as a child huddling in his room after his parents have
had a fight;
       As unable to intervene as a bystander watching a be-
      heading,
         Helpless,
         Thrown aside,
         Encompassing tension,
         Blanket of darkness,
         Ever growing, ever enveloping the soul.
Under that roof, family broken, divided, at a point of no return,
five years of built
       Up anger,
Screams echoing throughout the house begging to be released
from that prison of doom,
       Slowly waiting for death,
The air in there was heavy on our shoulders, people left to seek a
sanctuary to break
       Down and cry away from that brick menace,
Screaming, crying, and gnashing of teeth under that roof,
       Bearing down on four angry souls.
Vomiting up black-green suppressed hate,
        Haven for Madness inhabited by souls ridden by
      demons,
        Wallowing in the Stagnant Swamp of Willfully
      Discarded Memories,
         Leaving the built up anger in that bottle,
         Divided House,
         Bank of Negative Energy and

House of Mixed Emotions.

Religious Override

When she's around,
You can feel the fascism in the face.
If you don't believe,
Prepare to be damned to Hell
By her iron fist.
You can see her profound patterns.
Pattern of religion.
Pattern of change.
Pattern of brainwashing
And using the whip of God.
I see the sadness in the face.
Why does she keep on doing it?
Every two years
Her mind of absolute truth changes.
Visits to her house are like being
Under the rule of a totalitarian dictator.
I hear every time from her that I worship Satan.
Whatever.
She writes Bible verses on the floor,
I stare at her.
Does she enjoy this?
I see black rings and wrinkles

Around her eyes.
I think not.

Untitled

I don't know why this world keeps turning. I don't know. Why? Why me? Why? It's so hard. I have no idea. What? Who? What? Where? Why? How? Why does it matter? Who cares? This is bullshit. What the fuck is that. This is not happening. Is it? No, no, no. It is not no way. Why? Why? Why? It doesn't make sense. Why why why why why why why why why why why is it me? It is not it that is it, it is it that is the one that is not the one that the one asks why of the thing it does not understand about things which are not what of the what that is not answering the questions. I ask it for no reason the clock ticks just to annoy me and won't stop stop stop stop please stop, I won't ask again stop.

The Unattainable

Thou art troubled.
Art thou not?
Yes,
But to a passing eye
It cannot tell.
What idea doth have me in its spell?
This thing I cannot escape?
What is this thing that troubles thee?
I have pondered this thing many a time.
And why I cannot escape it
Escapes my scope of logic.
Canst thou think of other things?
No!
Mine eyes will not leave it.
The beauty of it all.
The shape and form
Doth captivate me.
I must have it.
But I don't know.
It might be but a fleeting fancy.
I've stayed up cold, dark nights
Wanting what I have not been able to achieve.

O!
What is this love?
This idea?
Why do I want it so?
Why do I want a beautiful girl
To feel
And share it with?
But what if it is but an idea?
Can I really attain it?
How I long for it.
How I long for a woman's touch.
Can you attain such?
I don't know.
I must try.
Even if
Love is made in the minds of others,
I want to make love
To her
In mine.
In ours.

The Illusion of Choice

These are times that try men's souls.
The path you choose to take
Alters your fate.
You may choose to care,
Or
You may choose not to care.
It makes no difference.
The path may be already set,
You just have to walk it.
Step by Step.
Wide is the gate and broad is the way
That leads to destruction.
Choose wisely.

Untitled

In my own little world, there is no bounds no limits. Whenever I want to I can just go there. there is no rules in my little world, I can do whatever I please because I am really not hurting anyone. All it really is is just one big work of fiction trailing on and on into infinity and beyond for all I know. My thoughts my feelings all of them jumbled together in one big story to belong to. This is my passion my passion is to write or read and go off into my own little world where no one can do nothing to me. Hell no. You ain't crackin' in there. Oh no. I'm psycho. Just trying to get my feelings out in words but not knowing how to express them or what to do in this world of stereotypes and weird intuitions. The things people conceive of each other are theirs and theirs alone. No one can take that away. Not if a million horses ride over your head and split it into two parts. Nuh uh. No one can take that shit away from you. No fucking way. Am I rambling. I'm rambling. What the fuck is going on in my head. OH shit. OH shit. So much to do. So much to contemplate. This is fucked up, fucked up I tells ya. Stupid bastard. Oh shit---

TICK

THIS is the time of DEATH.
This is the time of sleep.
This is the time of reflection.
When the world lay cold and white.
No beast doth roam in snow under leafless trees.
A sign of end but not hope lost.

Bare trees bring chills to thee;
The emptiness rampant.
But deep down you know,
Life springs again.
Death's grip lingers only so long.
As we look back on our choices,
Maybe our soul is washed white.

A sickle of ice falls to the ground and shatters.
It is no more.
A squirrel lies with a white blanket of death
Wrapped lovingly about its fur.
Time moves with no apparent care.
Take advantage of the slow time.

The sadness lingers only so long.
Ticks of the hand,
You can't go back.
Punch the clock and time still laughs.
Laugh back and know that you looked back
As you saw everything die.
You knew you wouldn't make the same mistakes
Once the warm sun
Melts the snow.

The World Unseen

The ever-growing eye
Watches.
All seeing.
All hearing.
All knowing.
His sympathy growing
As he watches
The piles of sickness
Burn.
The time draws close.
When the ever-growing hand
Will poke out the eye.
The eye's sympathy and knowledge
Will be lost,
Forever hidden in a
Crushed retina.
Flowers spring to life where
The eye lay blind and
Wet.
The dark times of the hand
Had come.
The eye knew

And again had sympathy
For the ones subject
To the palm's wrath.
Pain died and the eye
Cried no more.
The flowers died.
The world unseen.

Real

The thing that troubles us inside
The bubbling madness we can't hide
Glowing purple beacons reach the shore
Of reality's cold embrace
The nightmare land of shadowed face
Can there be absence of dark?
Or just absence of light?
Riding on the infrared wings of night
Soaring, observing your dreamscape
Dark figures and splashy red figments
The target is known
But not wanted
Blood-red dreams projected onto white eyes
Eyelids hang heavy
Holding onto the dream world
Scratchy writing on the wall
Rips the eye from the socket
The life you felt is unattainable
In this place
Your palms drip rancid images
The mark has been made
You never forget

That world is real

My Happy Thoughts

One hand is on the 16,
The other on the nine.
Everything I want
That couldn't be mine.
Been searching for the right line.
It's all in my mind.
The flowing hair,
The haunting, enchanting smile
Of one flaunting, daunting,
And unattainable.
The fall of the outstretched hand
Creates unknown wind through her hair.
Distantly I see that face, beautiful
And fair.
The goal and target
In this
Is known
And is wanted.
Trying to reach through the black veil
That malignantly covers my face.
The crash and crack of bone
As my hand smashes into

The brick barrier.
To break it down
Is possible
If I persevere
And the motivation holds.

The skull crack and shatter of glass.
Frustration is an impenetrable cloak
That I wear always.
To look down at the maze,
Is to see my path.
I can't find my way.
The mouth of the mountain
Cries with shrill laughter
At my trouble.
What is there to lose?
She slips from my grasp;
Swimming in the ever-growing
Dark gap.
Between me and my door
Is a crimson battlefield.
There is a battle to end all things.
I see my reflection in the green
Pool of vomit.
My past, present, and strife
The black whips of life
Grow as dreadlocks
Out of beauty's head.

Trapped in a group because of overrated stereotypes.
To break the cycle.
To take a stand.

To put your manhood out
Just to get your sac brutally sliced
With a jagged female snake-tongue.
Hissing and bile-spitting cock-teasing demons.
The succubus.
Your status is predetermined
And judged
By the sunken eye-masks of the blind light-eaters.
My label is not known but is there.
The busy knife-plunge to the heart
Leaves me wallowing in blood,
Vomit.
Two balls roll down the hall to be trampled.
Mucus and cum and vomit
Spewed out of one source
The human soul.
Acts and personality void
In the eyes of the Judges.
Have a heart,
We're all people.

Apart

The years of my existence
Have not yet been a hindrance
To my mind of chains and steel.
These sixteen years
      I've been
Out of luck sometimes
In years long since past,
But now in 2006
      I break the walls down fast.
The risks are not less taken
But before I had been fakin'.
Time has lost
And love has died
And the ropes they have been tightened.

The blows
And shots
And stabs.
I've seen it all go down;
Till the promise land is coming
I'll still be down here drumming
On my gooey hyperconsciousness.

The things that I love most,
And the things that tear my soul
Will not be of consequence
When the world is void and bare.
I think the time has come
Where we have to breathe our last.
What, my man, will you do
When the beast has come to snatch?

i fall into your rapture

i fall into your rapture
i am encapsulated
        by your wings of beauty
you Unlock me
do you wish to key my mind's world?
i am killed and resurrected simultaneously in your embrace
(piles
of
stones)

your presence is omnitextured
        glowing
                radiant
        sin
your heart is
a bundle
of
loving constricting tentacles
the things that i have done
and the things that i have Seen
are of no comparison
to your landscape

(oh the shapes)
lips bursting with flames of putrid
        beauty
(repulsive glamor)

the sword of your soul
grips my heart
but i will continue to
tread your
        Meadows
but your Shadow is penetrating

Blank Thoughts

dancing and dancing
spinning and spinning
      music
listening, i don't have to
      remember
don't have to
      think
when i listen,
i don't have to dream
      about you
because when i do
it's torture
knowing
you don't notice me

i look at you
you don't notice
it's a hook in my eye
i just want to talk
but i can't
separated
by self-inflicted barriers

which have power if i let them
i have no power

i think i will try
i don't
i fetalize into myself
my bubble
your bubble
rarely touch
much less embrace
burned by your face

cant just sit here
        try

Maybe

maybe
maybe i'll find love
    with a girl
maybe i'll find love
    with a boy
maybe
to me
love is love
i try not to limit
to find someone's beauty
that finds my beauty
if anyone thinks it's a small world,
try finding that person
the WORLD may be small
but
    there's a hell of a lot of people

Jazz Hole

The unspoken
Is what I cannot seem to break
What i cannot see
Hurts more
To slice in
Will be painful
But the alternative is to die
To limit myself
To stretch to a boundless environment
In which
      Absolute beauty
                  Is visible
Tear stains on the pages of my book
That I try to write
As best I can
If
In reality
I could pencil myself in
Where thoughts could be
      Transferable
But it cannot be
I only have the power

To write for my character
It is harder than
        The swish of a pen
        The words of a wand
        A portable gateway
It is harder
        To get to people's hearts
        To expose my heart
The passguard
Is not on my side
He keeps extending the gap
But alas,
The passguard is really
        Myself

Past histories
Shared Histories
Histories
        I am not in
Tidal wave
Blocks
Walls
Netting
Suspended in air
        Lost
And gasping for breath
The explosion of words
The endless string of
        Characters
That the mind outputs
Cannot be readily translated
But must be purged from the mind

To white
Maybe then they can be understood
Change
And
Longing
Is really what it says
But
Tragic sparkles fall
Around the eyes of the
Newly realized
The word new
The right move
The toss of a rock
The flash of an instant
Maybe
Last and uttermost
Freedom for pain
Rings must be shaped for
The right counterrevolution
There should always be
An uprising
Against the accepted
No
Damn the fickle hearted
Scratch at the door
'Til you have no nails and
You smell blood
The time
Is short
But endless
The meaning of the word try is lost
And the action is dormant

Timegasm

The dream
It is unfolding.
I have to start it now.
There is no time to waste,
Get it before it's gone,
Lost in a thought.
A memory
With denied access.
This instant
Will never come again.
Time is a sadistic
Forever.
Stroking itself
While others suffer
As it goes on
Leaving your chances behind
Charging you forcibly forward
While you are not ready
Going back is not an option.
Frozen in Time's memory
Forever used for it to get off.
Laughing and moving,

Constantly spanking you into submission
Like a disobedient lover.
Time penetrates and won't pull out.
Forever
Leaving its seed
        In your mind.

PART TWO

Tangled Light
Tentacles

Light

Snow is falling,
Darkness is gathering
In time and space between.
My mind and vision a blur.
Concept upon concept
Spoon-fed to a mouth
Which regurgitates every drop.
The mind and soul connected
Is daunting
As well as painful
To fathom.
It is hard
To be thrust into a world
Where in your own life,
You are the one making the least of the choices
That affects your death.

Beams of light
Stretched between mind and soul.
Knowing not the purpose,
Hinders the use
And to harness it,

Unthinkable.

Wings of White

In my world,
Sleep doth come but once a year.
I do sleep but once a day.
But that sleep,
Haunted and Hellish.
Ripped by dreams of
Death and Rape.
Protection does not come
In this barren wilderness.
My own mind betrays me.
And finds new ways to hurt me.

But soon.
When Time is gone and dead,
Sleep will come,
With broad white Wings.
That one single day.
And I will Sleep.
Like every night
Except,
This time,
The wing will be my

Protector.

Messiah

the religious following
of one so great
cannot be explained to the
Rational Mind
you must be a follower to know the power

if i were to become so Great
as that
i would Shed my earthly body
on this earth
and the fire that consumes
could not touch me
the fire would bow to me
and do My every command

And if I was to destroy the world
so be it
to make an impact on so many weak minds
is not a great feat
you just need a little hate

the hate that drives us

the hate that Consumes us
can only be understood if you've used it
tears will be shed freely when i shake the foundations
that people so easily Trust
the fear will run as the earth splits

they will all bow to me
when i have Descended upon
their predamned souls
it doesn't have to be me

they'll always find someone to follow
        blindly like moles

Untitled

I thought about you
As I was walking home
And I think about you now
But you don't know
Inside your dome
I can only imagine
What it's like
Think about letting me in

Standing on the outside looking in
Seemingly impossible for you to sin
Why can't our conversation
Last forever?
Cause
You shut the door
I distance myself
Screaming, crying on the floor
Thinking. . .
Help me. . .

Kileen
You don't know

You don't see enough of me
To realize. . .
That I'm in love with who you are
But you are so far

Time is blurred
And breaking me
Look and see
Your eyes
Open up to the noise
Everyone knows
'Cept you
I don't know
Or you just go with the flow
Trying to ignore

I'm getting kind of tired
With this clock
Existing just to mock me

Can't Crack

Lost in a dream
Time storms
I can't move
I'm gagged and bound
Lost, lost in time
It feeds off your pain
It feeds off your sorrow
And drinks your blood-red tears
Just to stay alive

I can't seem to crack
Through this invisible sarcophagus
I can't seem to crack
Time is stalking me
Consuming me
And makes it all come
Shattering around me

I know
Who you
Think you are
Look up at the sky

Stand and sigh
No portal there
Or ever will be
Stars are bright and lonely
Wings of time encircle me
Cannot seem to see
The fear is here

So you sit and
Wandering through this darkness
Then you fall
Infinity between
Unconscious and Soulconcious
But paralyzed
Surrender
In space and time
He tortures, whips, and
Consoles you -
But you know
He will never let you go

Night of Noise

Been out of town
Sometimes I forget
When I saw your face last
You're far away from me
Miles in between
I'm shadowed,
Cloaked in Darkness
And your light can't get to me

But when you turn your head
Open your bright eyes
And break into a smile
Letting your laughter break
The screams in my head

The night is noises
That I do not connect with you
Am I just a fool
Searching for your light?

So I stand and wandering
Through this darkness

Try to distinguish fact from fiction

You haven't called to me
I have to call to you
Cause I want to have you
And want to know you
And show you the world

Blinded by the fierce intensity
Pounding in my brain
Your image burned
Scarred forever
in my mind

You cannot leave me now
We still got time to share
The memory has to last

If we forget the past
Then we cannot write the future
I must choose to search you out

Untitled

This is now obsession.
Abandoning all reason.
And I hear the things they say,
And for my love I'll eventually pay
For something I do not have.
But my mind is not worth saving.

I know this makes no sense.
Between me and you I see the fence.
I don't even know you.
But nevertheless,
I feel as if you have my throat
Gripped as if you tethered my mind.
But I find
I can't block your face.
I can't stop this race.
I shouldn't want you so bad.
This is fucked up till the day I die.
I just need to say goodbye.

I know what I need.
I scream and bleed

As the night wraps in around me.
I just think about your face.
Then I remember my place
And the impossibility.
But tomorrow
I'll see your face again
Forgetting where I've been
Or where I'm going.
'Cause All I think about is you.

Help me break the chain.
That kills and scars my brain.
I smash and break the picture frame.
What's too much is her fame.
I don't fit that group.
Crash in this endless loop.
Burn the picture in my head.
I never knew your beauty.
So release me now.
This is never going down.

It doesn't matter anyway.
Doesn't matter that it's today.
I cannot get away.
The scar is too deep.
I would only weep.
Do you not see?
The mark she made?
I cannot let go now.
She may not know now.
She may not care.
But I'm not going nowhere.

I'll just keep on dreamin'
Till the day is gone.

PART THREE

Rejecting a Surrogate Reality

The Little Death

Through life I'm always dying
but I will always keep on striving
forever on toward death

In death I will be living
forever in the present
infinity decomposing
on a Time-Darkened sky

My face is being smudged
The paint brushed off the canvas
Reality comes when light fades
and dreams emerge

Operation Dartboard

Operation dartboard is in production.Time is against me or us. I don't know if I can beat this fucking clock because the now bleeds into the past and the past bleeds into the future. Giant red putrescent shit coughed up from the one thing that is supposed to be trusted is not comforting to a person who wants to see the white wings outstretched, waiting to comfort. All these fucking pictures don't make any fucking sense, it is just a wash of colors plastered to a wall already covered with luminescent grief. Manifest in the walking shit is the epitome of social elite fucks pissing and shitting their way up the social ladder when we are down there getting rained on by foul pasteurized condescension. Every sexual device is not used for pleasure. It is just used because we fucking have to. No one says we have to but the unspoken purple fog shows all the invisible truths; those truths that kick us to the ground. Breaking our pearl teeth on the curb. That is sexually arousing to this elite. Constantly ejaculating hate and mockery on the less fortunate; leaving us wallowing in their semen of failure. These are the fucking cocksuckers that want to control our very existence. We must break out of these social stereotypes and show those fuckers we ain't takin shit from those that feel they have the gift of light shining out of their raw and bleeding anus. When we come to any conclusion, we never know or give a fuck how we came to it.

Twisted Torment

The dartboard has fallen.
Just let it lie.
Even though I sigh,
It is over,
It is done;
Fuck it all.
The world is too damn big
To just think of one.
This twisted torment has to end.
It ends now!
The picture is eradicated.
No more goal,
No more target.
I don't care.
It's all absurd.
It's all been make-believe.
Try to break the tether.
It is hard.
But my mind is set.
Just let it go.
Let it come.
I don't care.

It's not worth it.

Surrogate Wall

This is just a surrogate reality.
Then why do I feel the way I do?
The gravity of the black
Multiplies exponentially.
It means I can't escape.
The blood drips and is ripped
From my outstretched arms.
Yelling and screaming in
The smoke-drenched purple
Of the encrypted life.
It is all stuffy,
Fake
False
Fucked up.
Outside my wall.
Or inside.
Surrogate both.
Nothing is worth the suffering
Of the hate-bludgeoned
Love-sick puppy.
I wallow endlessly in this
Putrid liquid shit.

Time and time again,
Thought after thought
Nothing makes sense
You need wings
to get to me,
Over my wall
But when you come crashing over,
I'll be waiting to hand you a brick.

The Breath of Glass

The try might fall to abyss,
For all that my life is worth.
Do it for the moment of flash -
Blinding light pushes the demons aside.
That won't help a bit
Because the future is nothing
In this moment.
Glass falls to the sand
Here in this broken land.
Mind of now is unreal to the spoken.
Fervor is lost in the emotional miscarriage
Pulling life from the open
Mouths of constant grief;
Flowing to the collective shit
That is all people.
This mindset is hard to spurn,
But now it's my turn
To live
To breathe
To strive
For a better tomorrow.
To feel again what the waste has taken from me.

All there is to do is
To say fuck it.
Make the pain go away.
'Too late' is a cop out.
You know what to do.
Don't focus on what you don't have.
Just take it.

Cloud Carriage

I don't want to be who I am.
Kill the person that's inside.
Myself has become a cliché;
Predictable.
I don't want it that way.
I have to change me,
To become what I envisioned.
It is within my power to do so.
But the blackness closes in
And I lose the strong mind.
So I fall and am suffocated
In the madness of the predictable life.

Time and Time I try.
But the try is not good enough
To pull me through
The gateway to the sky.
The sky of her face.
And when I do try,
My face is ripped by
A rusty hook;
Leaving me with a jagged scar

Forever reminding me of my failure.

Trash and the human condition.
But is it just that way
Because that is how we are programmed to think?
That drama in one's life is coveted?
Depression is glamorous?
Why does it matter?
How I feel is how I feel.
Time is trapped in an endless
Hopeless spiral
Where I never know if
I can better myself.

Colorful Darkness

Time is dead in this waste --
Land has never been killed.
Everything is made;
Everything is thought up.
Everything of loathing and disgust.
Where the mind has turned to dust,
Here where everything is broken;
Where women hurt,
And women desert.
Nothing can heal the wounds the
Monsters have made.

Everything is burning;
Consumed by fire
For eternity;
undying.
All things considered,
Nothing matters because it is a world
Of endless pain.
But Time stops
And glass shatters,
Piercing; blood flowing

To the sand.
Nothing means anything.
Nothing matters
When the dreams are ripped by
Monsters, death, and rape.

In the world of colors
That just consist of darkness,
Nothing can be seen except for
Grotesque beauty.

Laughing

There is no escape from my prison.
This place where I am blind to everything except
Black.
And where I'm deaf to everything except
Screams.
I cannot trust my dreams
For that's what they show me.
I am being eaten by the succubus;
Evil two-headed women who taunt me.

Burning hyenas circle me
And laugh at me.
I cannot escape this desert,
It is infinite
Because I made it
And stocked it with demons.
These hyenas: the burning demons of
My Soul.
Giggling as they tear apart my heart
And feed it to the women of my nightmares.
They are laughing at me --
These creatures I have made --

Are laughing.

Forever living
Forever dying
In the moment.
I am forever tired,
But in this moment,
I wish to wake.

Fuck Shit

Why is everything not worth living for? Why am I so fucked up? Why am I so cowardly? Fuck all this. Nothing will ever get better. I will never be able to better myself so fuck this world I really don't want to live as myself anymore but I am not strong enough to change so I might as well die because everything sucks just take a knife and put it to my throat cut it purple just pours out because I am just purple kill me I can't fuck fuck this shit fuck it

TIME

T remendous waste I can't escape
I ncessant numbers digitally burned
M ust the steady tick drive us mad?
E ventually all of it will cease

Touch the Cerebrum

Something I wish was growing.
Something I wish was there
The void shows what's missing.
The touch of a woman.
The touch of beauty.
The hips, breasts and ass.
Is that all that counts?
Will that fill the void?
Are they all fucking bitches that tease us?
I will rip those girlie whinings out of ---
What was your phone number again?
THEY ARE ALL THE SAME.
They will NEVER be tame.
However, I don't know what's in the moment when I live it.
Everything falls in place like broken train tracks.
Run for the hills.
I can't wait to shake this baby up.

Black Mist

Trapped in this land full of liquid colors;
Nothing is real except for the words
That have no meaning except in the
Moment they are purged from the constipated mind.
What is real is never found
In this blistering heat.
The relative world is blinded
        by the cosmic joke which is mankind.
We are just here to satisfy God's
        sadistic nature.
But the hate rubs off
And the human race is dying.
We are falling.
We cannot see any of the signs
        pointing to catastrophism.
It doesn't really matter if we die.
We know where we are going:
Continuously down.
Caught in the death spiral
        of my emotions.
I cannot see what will happen
        because Time is forever.

The Cult Machine

I must get it started because the machine won't wait for the mind to boot up because I have forgot the password to the clouds. I cannot move farther until the wings shed their feathers to the ground already covered with blood of the seraphim. Things don't make sense to be real because what is real right now are the spikes driven through the chest of the cosmos. Out there nothing matters and all is known and nothing is needed to know. I cannot determine how the climactic moment when the black mist meets the purple fog because because grown men fall on their face before the portal of sin because they are too afraid to step through the door of decision. This marks a turning point in the history of suicide because the attempt is to achieve life.

Lives of the Dead

Souls alight
And souls aflame
Been soaking in the righteous blame
Climbing the mountain of fame
The fame of someone no one knows
Death and life are indistinguishable
From the dreams that are welcomed
Welcomed with open arms
Dreams bring the dead to life
And Stories are forever
A true story of a life never lived
An interactive illusion
One that you've invented
False undeniably real sensations
Felt without moving
Living without opening your eyes
For you, this is Truth
Eternal bliss
Floating between
Waking and Dreaming
Always hoping and always dying to live
To live your life after you're gone

Purple Fog

Everything is not as it appears in this world. Underneath everything is something hidden. Something dark. And it is waiting to spring forth from its prison. This prison that constricts and crushes. But everything changes. Everything can be discarded for something new; something better. I can't say that I know everything and every way to change oneself. I don't. However, things must continue forward everyday. Everyday we must strive and live and breathe for a better world. What is predictable and what is shocking? Does anything shock anymore? Is everything predictable and mundane? To change from the sporadic to the logical is a difficult task if the brain is filled with howling demons. I can't find a place where they belong. I can't find a place where they can benefit me. Is it possible to take something destructive and make it productive? The stomach fills up with unwanted purple smoke. But it needs to be blown away and cleared so that what can be seen is the truth. But what you find is the purple smoke is covering the black mist. But the black mist cannot be cleared as easily as the purple smoke was. Everything must come and go on the wind. Fantasy, Truth, Reality, and Dreams are all intricately connected within a person's internal fog. The fog that intertwines everything with itself. I can't see what's beyond the mist. I don't want to see what's beyond the mist because I know that it is not what is desirable. Everything is snowballing downhill, picking up speed, and it cannot be stopped without causing some destruction and some death. Is it possible to have a death be not in vain? In Time everything becomes falsified. In Time everything becomes purple and clouded. The memory fades and imagination sets in. Everything is hidden by a woven cloak that is only seen by the ones who are blind. This cloak that is intricately patterned with silk and blood. The screaming of the nullified shatters all of the heat that surrounds the banks of the flesh. The flesh cracks and the mind breaks in sharp fragments of the creation that has spawned all of the hidden tragedies. Nothing can happen without a trial. Trials of temptation and trials of crashing down around the souls of the corrupted. The fire and the shit pouring down like rain covers every inch of the plane of thought. No idea can ever be determined without some consequence. These consequences being the production of the tired lives of all of the apostles of the cold and dusty world. I can't seem to see beyond the horizon. This horizon infinitely strangles the correlation between life and wine. Every time a shot gets fired a little petal falls into a warm pool of honey; honey that has become bitter with the blood of the weak. The mind is a powerful tool that can be used as a scythe or a pool of water. It is so tiring to be here when nothing is going on around you. You look into the faces of the righteous and you see nothing. The faces are vacant; and the ones that are supposed to help and comfort are never there when the sky rains down parts of the sun. Will it always shine down on us? Will it always be there for us? No. It was never there when I was buried under the purple fur of the matriarch. Everything dies but everything lives. Life is what is wanted. Isn't it? Isn't life what is good and what is necessary to become the creature one wants to become? But everything fails and everything succeeds. But success does not come to those who only see the black mist. You must extract what is desirable from the black mist and walk on until the sun rises over the horizon. And if the sun does not come. If the sun deserts you for some other equation of time and space, you must be your own sun; shine the way through the darkness and find what is purple. I know that things change. And I know that things stay the same. What is wanted is to DO what is wanted. But we fuck up and everything goes to shit when the sun dies and the moon reigns over the barren land of the enchanted domain where the fragmented live. Nothing happens until you fuckin do something about it. Life only is worth living if you create it that way.

PART FOUR

Hopeful Despair

Tide

How does the moon control the tides?
Why does the tide move in and out?
Like everything on the wind.
In and out,
Ceaselessly moving and ceaselessly changing.
Does the tide signify hope
Or despair?
The trick of the moon shows everything below in a blue shadow.
The tide can bring me pearls
Or the tide can bring me death
Decomposing on the beach,
Forever under the watchful eye of the moon.

Will the tide ever stop?
Will the tide ever give up?
When the moon fails to shine its blue down on the sea
Then what?
If I cannot see the tide moving in and out
And in and out,
Does that mean it has ceased to move?
Even if the moon ceases to instruct the waves,
The wind still carries my dreams on the tide.

Will the tide ever die?
Can death come to aspects of life that seem unchanging?
All these things instruct other forms of life.
If one dies, must all the rest cease to be?
Does one action always affect the majority?
Does Time affect the waves,
The moon?
The blue peace of eternity in the sky
Shows me the way toward hopeful despair.

Schism from the Dark

Try to stop this from taking over. The mind has constituted a schism from the time of the dark. The time when people drop like flies. When their intestines fall to the ground in heaps of pig guts. What does everything mean when it is written on a wall of blood? This lifeblood that seeps from the pores of the damned. Who would ever bathe in entrails? The Dying Fetus of music scars the soul and the eardrums. I can never understand anything that goes on in this world because everything drips black menstrual blood off of the contours of the moon.

Forced Cranial Exposure

Force the time that wanders through everyday existence
Destined to be neither dead nor alive through all of the
      expanses of the tempted
Tragic flagrance of floral canopies atop an
      ever present rainbow of reflection
The reflection which is myself and told to
      nothing other than my own train
Trucked and fucked through everything
      I have no control over
In this life

Cracked in half and split from stem to spine
I cry for the world to end in the attractive
      embrace of empathy
I don't know if I can top this
I don't know if I can cure all of the
      heartache and diseases that plague our time
This time that needs no attention other than
      what breaks the skin of the neck of endurance
Clock-knocked and shit-talked
      all the days that laugh at your pain
Trying and trying to control the sleepless days of silence

Bowing to all the flowing blood from the
      ever luminescent sparkle dustless
Crammed in a room where you only fit
      when the legs are broken under you

I can't seem to break the temptation to claw
Claw from the now to the present and
      crouch and gasp in the darkness of space
The spacing happens only if I know that I can and I know
That Nothing ever happens in this dusty land
      crawling with living staples
Ingrained in my mind is all the meaningless,
      all the effervescent colors of the night
My eyes fall out and I no longer know what is good for me
All I see is nothing and darkness and the
      loneliness consumed in time
And Time doesn't stop for me and
      my clouded resting place full of dead christmas

Security

The ever-growing questions of my own psyche
cannot be answered by me.
But I try my hardest to find the Truth,
Even when the out-reaches of my family extend their Love.
And some tell me the answer can only be found
        within the majesty of God,
But for whatever reason, I reject it
        and crawl to the place where Dust encircles my eyes.
It is so difficult with the things I know and
        the things I think I know.
But the illusion of reality must stay in place for security.
Because security is the most important thing,
Right?
I cannot blink, because if I do, the lights will go out
        and the Universe will turn to nothing,
And I will be back at square one.

All That's Left

The creation of darkness grows ever present
From the soul of darkness
The soul of hate
The soul of injustice
Everything of mockery vomited from the past,
      to the present, to the---
Time---
Time is the key to knowing
To go back
To travel through
To change what the outcome would---
Would it be worth it?
Would anything fucking change?
Would anything fucking work?
Or would the batteries have to be perpetually changed?
To be bludgeoned
To be bludgeoned by all the cruelty and malice that
      comes from the black parasitic heart
        of remembrance
Of all the memories of long past
All the memories, bad, good, happy, sad---
Bloodshed

Shedding tears, blood dripping through fingers outstretched
Peeking through to find the sun through all the mist of Loathing
Loathing time, space, matter, and my own existence
Clawing for now to be better
For now to be change
For now to be what I envisioned
-----But nothing
---And nothing---
Ever works out
      ---EVER---
      ---NEVER---
      ---EVER---
Completely fucked in time
And shat out to the darkness
Continually labeled to rot
And fester till the dogs decide to rape me
To rape me of all my want
All my dreams
All I hoped to become
The present is overrated
And the past is condemned
All that's left is the future
The future I know is continually crawling with anal parasites
I can't see!------------------
I can't see!------------------------
Fuck me!--
Fuck Me till I die---
Everything is fucked--
All that's left to do is
      DIE!--

Red Box

To talk of everything
To bridge everything over the snows of crying
I am buried in snow
Snow soaking into my ears and eyes
Cold
Cold as the sky that lights the sea on a winter's night
Winter
Forever winter
Forever twisted in the frost of malnourishment
No food
I'm so hungry from my hiding place in this cave of ice
Drips fall on my hood and
My sleeves are crusted with snot
Dried mucus from my heart
I don't know if I have one
A heart that is
Maybe numb
Maybe to become numb to the pain
Numb to the want
Numb to the ice
All I want is warmth
Warmth to encircle me

And encompass me with Golden comfort
But then I remember
My heart is crusted with ice

Sealing Wax

I stare into the abyss of longing
And I feel hot wax drip from my tear ducts
Butterflies
Butterflies clean as my mind is sealed and burned
        with hot irons of loneliness
But nothing gets sealed
Nothing gets done
Nothing gets accomplished
When my father plunges a jagged, rusty fillet knife
        into my chest cavity
He slices open my soul and sifts through my organs
Searching for one that beats
One that feels
One that cares
Something for him to eat
To consume
As my arteries hang through his teeth, he grins and laughs
As he removes the one thing left with feeling
Now I'm anesthetized as I lay on the white operating table
Dad is still hovered over me
My own blood drips from his lips
It sizzles and burns as it hits my skin

I try to scream but can only move around
       the stump in my mouth
The gaping hole in my chest must be stoppered
Is it?
Because in a flash of an instant
Father is gone
And Hot Wax
Drips from the vacancy
In my chest

What I Need

Tremendous waste of time always consumes everything I see.
I cry to the winds of my mother's hair
And wade in the waters of Truth.
But the truth is hidden
And I am blinded by myself.
Tracking
And running through a shattered staircase
Slicing my tendons.

I stumble as the red rain drips acid from my open wounds.
I get ripped and gorged and ravaged by all things time
        and clouded by the skyman.
I can't
I always can't
Because now is the toothless fighters caught
        inside the hearthouse clawing at freedom.

Freedom is the key.
Freedom is the key to be liberated from
        the household of conquest and fascism.
I can see the storm coming.
The storm that will tear the church to shreds

And leave the dark spirits victorious.
I know now what must come.
I know now what must be fulfilled.
The prophecy of sin is death.
But what must suffice is the aspect
        of clouded dreams of murdering and raping.
My eyes are bloodshot and what I need is water.

The Antichrist Scenario

People never see what is really in front of them.
It's a world corrupted with sin.
We are only fed what the media wants us to see.
What is wrong with a society
     that gets pleasure from the grotesque?
We only see the world through this mist of blood.

We all bow to Satan.
We don't love Jesus or the Cross.
We only see our personal pain.
So it's time to lay down our arms and give in to the Darkness.
Evil is the only thing that lives.
Evil is the only thing worth fighting for.
It is so easy to see Lucifer
But where has our Lord gone?
Has he forsaken his children?

The only thing left is to blow out my brains.
Let the blood spray like cleansing rains.
My skull fills
My skull fills with blood
Blood of the Raven

Of the Time
Of the Crime
We all committed against our Creator.
Can we fuck Jesus?
If we can,
We already have.

Why can't you see
That the only one worth worshipping is the Fallen One?
To tie a woman to a bed is ceremonial.
To insert the blade into the chamber of life
Is what has to be done to
Be accepted by the Prince of Darkness.
Draw blood from every orifice and
Bask in the acceptance of Sin.

Why must we kill God?
Because without him, it's all about
Us
And our selfishness.
But it's not about us
It's about
The Prince of Darkness
And how to bow.

I fucked the cross and
Raped the tomb
And pissed on the spot where
He was buried.
We have
We all
We know

We have
Done that.
We need to know
The cross is burning.

All this time we live in
The wastelands of our souls.
As I trek on through the dark spirals of forgotteness
The only comfort I get is from these Demons.
The only pleasure I get is from these Demons.
They rake my skin with their jagged claws.
I cum as my naked body is whipped by bone tipped leather.
The crown of thorns is pressed into my scalp.
Until all I can see is blood.

As I walk through this world with my crown of thorns,
Dragging a splintered cross over my own grave
Which is boiling with sewage and monsters of my mind.
But when the crucifix is on the ground,
I lay nailed in the wood by screws out my spine.
Blown by a vampire maiden as my lumbar
        bleeds on my holy wood.
I am the Antichrist.
We are the Antichrist.
We need to know that.

Is the harvest here?
All the corn,
All the Christians to slaughter.
America,
Where Jesus Freaks are scorned and
Triple Six Mafia is worshipped.

To eat my own heart and bile from the intestines of Truth.
It is Time.
It is always Time
To Rape everything.
We constantly rape the name of God.
The Bible becomes laughable
When society views Christians as crazy.
God must be just lazy.
All this violence.
All this sadness.
God doesn't give a fuck.
He can get on his knees
And suck.

Blasphemy.
This is blasphemy.
But I don't give a shit
Because the hooks of rusty demon chains
        are imbedded in my ankles.
Pulling me around.
Controlling.
Because I like it.
Because I like to rebel.
Because I like to scream "FUCK GOD!"
Before my tongue is cut out by gremlins.
So I walk through life
Dragging chains.
Raping.
Torturing.
Fucking mutilated skulls dug up from the graves of the saved.
This is evil.
This is the Antichrist.

America is the Antichrist.

And I love it. . .

Cosmological Insurrection

Clouds fly above the earth in a pattern of wind currents
        as the landscape underneath changes
From the Compass of a changing society
        that sees things differently and through
                their own personal haze
I don't crack
I blaze on through this world
Tearing the searing hearts of fire from this
                world of mystics
And finally see what is truly beyond the stars
I see what is truly beyond the Authority
I see everything how it really is and what I must do
To bask in the glory of a completed and
        varnished frame of wood
The smell of fresh cedar
And the sound of crisp leaves
Is all I hear when the soft wind
        silently blows the grass through the
                Golden winds of change
But I know that hibernation only lasts so long
And the sun comes out again after the long freeze
The warmth returns again to the bright landscape

And white wisps fly through the atmosphere
        in cyclic currents of steadiness
What we must do is peel off our melting flesh
            and reveal the scarred tissue
But not shun it
Model it
And caress it
Love it and cherish it
Laughter is only a cut to the ear,
        but scars can be beautiful if we are not ashamed
Gash my heart and it will just uncover the fire therein
Eviscerate me and what will be left is intense light
Blazing through to the clouds above me
                rocketing toward the stars
In a spiral of longing
Our persistence may not carry us above the cosmos,
But we can and will set sights toward the skies

GODDAMNIT

Ow, fuck, the sun burns my eyes as I stare straight into the fire.
I can just feel it as my retina melts away.
I cannot determine why I inflict this self mutilation on myself.
Oh, God, No!
Why must it happen this way when
        the sun is setting beyond the mist?
I can't fucking finish if the sun leaves and the moon comes up.
I will be left with these horrible, steaming,
        half-fried orbs in my skull.
I gotta finish, where's my blowtorch.
Ahh, ahh, why, it burns, aww my brain, I can't, no.
I pull the flame away as I feel boiling liquid
        drip down my cheeks.
I can't see... but the fire... and the burning... and
Oh FUCK OH MY GOD IT BURNS
WHY GOD WHY
It's all gone
My world has been swallowed by
        the herpes infested cancerous whore I can't see
But, maybe, when I burn the world from in front of me,
The tick of time will slow,
And I can make my own fire.

Asphyxiated By a Serrated Cross

I feel something clogging my throat and I can't tell if it is
      mucus or blood.
But I find it is piercing through my stomach
      and out of my anus.
I can't see it but I feel solid, dense matter
      forcing my jaws open.
I grab it and I rip.
I rip it up and out,
As splinters are left in my trachea.

I lay here, paralyzed in my bed,
Helpless to the onslaught of doctors and holy men.
I am wounded
And I cannot speak because
My throat has been lacerated by this twisted cross.
But they still hover, close their eyes, raise their hands,
And speak words over me.
Even though it makes the holes grow.

Always told of the One way,

The One Power,
Or I will lay sizzling in this lake of fire
FOREVER.
But, as I stand here,
I look up and see two paths splayed out before me,
They both are overgrown with flowers and the trees
That canopy the path sing beautiful music
As I walk down the left.

Pull the Hammer Back

I awake on a cloud,
And notice the surrealism of severed wings
      flying through the air.
I wobble but do not fall as wisps of smoke blow my hair
In a comforting pattern of perfumed kisses in a rainstorm.
I feel the bliss of a star forming and a moon falling
Into this world of perfection.
This is where the saints go to die.

But I realize that nothing is all right
And not all the dirt has been scrubbed from these walls.
I behold a massive sheet of white cloth swinging to and fro
Through the puffy clouds.
I feel sudden heat coming from below me
      as the cloth shudders back.
I hear something, but it is muffled by cotton and clouds.
I lay down on the cloud and look up at the long tube of cloth
And imagine, as if in a dream, the strongest part of persuasion.
It is hot, steaming metal
      pressed to the vulnerable part of the skull.
I close my eyes and listen as the hammer is pulled back by this
Malevolent giant.

I let out a gasp of realization and everything comes into focus
As my retinas turn white and my mind is clamped in a Book.
There is no decision,
Persuasion deals with the force of a projectile
        penetrating the skull.

Do you kiss the hand that delivers the pressure to your brain,
Or protest, and let the hammer rip?

Just Here, Just Look

It is so hard to grab the hand that is lost in the mist.
The hand is not reached out towards me.
I grasp and claw but the hand is so far away.
And it is no use to try because she'll just brush my fingers away
And hold another hand, not my hand
So I curse my hand and snap my fingers
Until I am satisfied with the shattered bone sticking out.
What the fuck?
The beauty is not meant for me because I
Cannot allow the soft down of a bird to cradle my cuts.
My cuts drip everything I have ever dreamed of.
I cannot stop the flow of syllables falling from my split wrist.
My lips are sewn together and they freeze and burn
From lack of use, lack of want.
She pulls her fingers through her hair,
The hair I will never touch.
Over the spirituous eyes I will never peer lovingly into.
Why must it sear and burn for me to realize the void,
The void of beauty, warmth, a soft touch, a simple...
In this world of nothing where I am forced celibacy,
I try to break the film around my heart.

Obligatory Paramour

Kiss me, beautiful.
If you do not, I shall turn into a despicable frog
Covered with warts and putrid to the eyes.
I shall be a reject and unloved by all.
Little children will scream as they see my horrid eyes
        bulging from my face.
But, I ask you now, before I become a Thing,
Will you not shower your love on a simpleton?
Or will you clench your silky, white, slender fingers
        around my throat
And squeeze the love out of me,
With your succubus hand?
Dost thou?
Dost thou look upon my being as a wretch?
I know that "Real beauty is found within" is just
        something ugly people say,
But why must you thwart me with your stringy locks of fire?
O, I look upon thine beauty as a shadow,
A sweeping wind passing me by with a laugh and no eyes.
I canst see your eyes, because therein thou hast
        emptiness of putrid waste.
Because your life is wasted in the heat of the game,

As you flaunt and saunter around in your tight things---
Bah!
I see thee not!
I want thee not!
Because I have something far greater,
Tis not the false beauty from within,
But the wings from without that allow me to enrapture
Your being and swamp thou with steaming atrocities.
Waste not, for I shall be there for you,
Well, only until your beauty is gone.
But nonetheless, I am aroused by you.

BITCH

You are a fucking bitch, okay?
Don't you know it?
I smell it on your rancid breath, you whore.
I can't fucking stand you.
You with your short, golden hair that is as false as your smile,
I can't touch you, much less to smack you
Because I cannot stand that stench and the white,
 billowy cancer pouring from
  your nostrils.
Hell, no, even though you have cancer,
 I don't really see you suffering,
But you must be because your stare is like a
 boxing glove to the jaw.
Fuck you!
You know what, you have succeeded and won this war
 that you have forged and designed
for yourself through these bitter winter snows.
I can feel your frost biting at me and driving me
 farther and farther away from the man I
  thought I knew.
You did this, I know you did!
And you can't hide it through the "I miss you"s.

I see your cunt-faced lies, you twisted, soulless bitch.

When you first crawled into this dormitory of comforting love,
        teddy bears were what I
                    could fall back on.
But you were right about creating your own world
        and you did just that,
You brought the winter freeze into what I thought was safe.
So now I lean back and I don't feel soft stuffed animals,
I just feel razor-sharp icicles piercing my flesh and I continuously
Walk around with frigid piercings that don't melt.
You tore out the branches of this family tree
        until there was just a leafless trunk,
Where you sit Queen on the top and control the roots.
You laugh that obnoxious laugh that sounds like a
        fucking rooster dying,
You are the most scummy skanky whore ever to tear up a family.
God knows what diseases you are crawling with
        when you lay naked on a party boat,
Giving your body to Whatever flapping penis
        slaps you in the face.
You always have,
Open your legs and let the Cockroaches crawl in,
        until is splits another branch of the tree.
Who knows, Whatever may be me...

Did You Know Pill Rhymes with Kill?

Everything is solved by a round, white tablet.
When I see unicorns prancing into a lake of endless orgies,
Everything is solved by a round, white tablet.
I can't see my face because my friend Oscar
      melted his shoes on some hot coals in the woods,
           and the Newscasters suspect something about me.
I cannot sit still in class,
     my foot taps and I drum out Korn on my desk.
Add Adderall to my list of suppositions.
It works!
Well, if you actually need it.
But parents continually leap straight for the pharmacy.
Just get the diagnosis.
You pay the bills, Father, he won't say no.

How am I?
I am chemically well,
Forever high on a wave of fluoxetine
     and immersed orgasmically in a bubble bath of
        hydrochloride.

Everything is solved by a round, white tablet.
Abilify me and my friend Billy,
        we snuggle up close in bed when I'm lonely.
zac is on the Pro football team at my school.
Daddy, do you want me to meet him?
Give me a transparent, orange canister
          to cover my penis from my brothers.
Is it a disease?
Am I Oriented to be cured?
Am I wired wrong?
There must be something missing in the Oceans of nudity
          where my gray matter meets
                the Straight.
Fix me with something white and hard down my throat.

Just Try It

My grandpa thinks that guys can't be Bi.
I say,
Sweat me,
Caress me,
Lick me up and down.
I can see different pictures of beauty
      swirling in and around my mind.
I see round, succulent breasts atop a slender body
      that holds the house of new life.
And I want to be inside, how I would love to be over those hips.
But I also see toned abs, sweaty pecs of steel,
      rock hard glutes, and a perfectly tan cock.
What's wrong with that?
The beauty is evident in both.
Trying to tie my tongue around the tongue of my muse.
I see her laying, exposed on my bed
      with her lips of lust, wanting entrance.
But I cut away and see a muscular beast of a man
      stoking himself by my side.
I step back and kiss the man as my muse watches, wet and eager.
Over top,
In out,

Moaning,
Sweat pouring,
Ginsberg knew what it was about:
"Cock and endless balls"
The pleasure is like a blinding light coming from heaven down
        to illuminate the grace of
            the human anatomy.
Limited just to one side?
Absurd.
I have my sturdy athlete and my feminine angel,
Double the pleasure, double my sin.
Sin me,
Penetrate me.

Gramps, I *have* been with a man and a woman.
Alone, then together.
Call it what you want,
Bi,
Questioning,
Experimenting,
Anything at all.
You think that only women can be Bi.
Huh?
Watch me.
Lick me,
Bind me,
Tame me,
Fuck me.
Hold me.
Hold me in your arms forever,
So I will never be lonely.

Man or woman really doesn't matter.
Can't you see that all I want is a beautiful body to rub against.
The time has come to put aside our inhibitions,
And become everything Taboo.
I can say what I want,
Do what I want,
Fuck who I want.
I can stretch, like a balloon to every corner
        of the sphere of consciousness and existence.
Let me see it all,
Bring it all to me.
Let me touch it,
Experience it,
If just once.
Explore,
You may find you like it,
You may find you love it.
Be something you are not and push the tradition
        out of the bounds of conventionality
And spread life,
Make life your lover as you spread her and enter in at lightspeed.
I think I love it.
Watch me if you can,
All eyes on me.
Guys, man, paint your faces, swirl in dresses.
Girls, shave your heads.
It doesn't have to be the same,
Living can be like skydiving every minute,
Just hug me and we'll see
Where our connections will lead us.

My Heroin

The darkness is not pushing, more infests my mind.
I have walked into the cavern willingly
        and dug continuously deeper,
Forever quagmiring myself into this.
So I can't really complain about anything.
But,
Sometimes,
I can't stand myself, I want to slash the mirror
                with my jagged nails.
But,
In distant flashes of instants, I can't get enough of myself.
The darkness is innocent,
And it seems like it is just the creative unharmful
                that slowly walks
Into your brain but does not manifest into a parasite.
But I am hindered by myself, my worst nightmare.
I look at the broken rungs of my ladder
        and they have words written there:
Faggot,
Wacko,
Psychopathic pervert.
And I fall,

Seeing myself being raped by a twisted Fetus,
That all adds to the broken rungs sometimes.
Help me,
Save me from myself.
But I do love it.
Even though the words,
Queer,
Perverted sicko,
Crazy,
Sink into my brain from time to time,
I must see it as the darkness I want to be, I guess.
I best break to freedom and the red, white and blue,
And shout to the world all my rights and how I love this place
And hate this place.
And how I kiss a stubbly cheek,
And how I finger the clit.
I can do that here,
I do it to try and forget,
Forget I was born being
raped.
Raped by the twisted spider
        that was called into being upon my birth.
Maybe that's why I crave everyone's eyes.
I want their pupils trained on me.
That's what I thrive on,
That's my drug.
It makes me see stars and sparkles and love
        that I once thought never to be mine.
Come up on stage and bask in my radiance
        in this transcendent moment of bliss
Where all sex dissolves and everything comes down to
                erotica.

The twisted Fetus won't slow me down this time, baby,
I am headed toward the stars,
Where the cameras are fixed forever
        on what I can create in my mind.
I see my life now, a waterfall glistening with sparkle makeup,
I am glamorous.
No drugs for me now,
The camera's my heroin.

PART FIVE

What the Blind Shall See

Some Shallow Dream

Lights, Camera, Action
Time falls away like leaves on an evergreen landscape
Every time I die I seem to escape a little bit
I lose a little of myself
I gain a piece of pain
Spirals of lust and longing and dreams
I can't seem to grasp on to anything worth anything
Worthless words and worthless promises
Broken by lies and swung by hate toward the abyss
Hanging by the neck is perpetrated by normal people
It's all for the sake of love
Why can't I love and then lose myself
  to swirling roses of perfumed curls
I am rejected by what I really want
No like-minds
No love, all hate
All narrowness and intolerance
Who wears the skirt and who wears the pants
I wear neither when I'm behind the camera
I shoot what I see
And what I feel
Strip me of all religion of all faith

And leave me with nothing
A skeleton with nothing but a heart
To be taken by the first who wants it
Who wants it?
It seems I am going to be here for a while
Waiting, lonely in this dialog of three that leaves me be
With my own thoughts
All move away
All move away from me
Fine, be your way of disgust, of filth, of putrid loathing
I hate you
For your hate
What I want is unachievable in this place
Let me fly away through the sky to a faraway place where
I can be myself and have the freedom and the time
To be outrageous
And have some fun
And share my love
With someone who appreciates me for who I am
God knew that I would never be
      the one that bends over to take it
Without argument
He knew
Why must I cry with no end in sight for this madness
Tangled in the roots of words
And the branches of thoughts
I can't get them out in any other way
I always sound stupid
Help me to realize what is me in this forgotten world
Of nothing where the only thing that survives
      is pain from this useless religion
If the Lord is so sweet

I can taste him like melting chocolate on my tongue,
But once I have consumed it, it is gone forever
Lost in the black whole of time
I have always wanted what I cannot have
And that never stopped me from going for it
Don't tell me to stop
Don't analyze my motives
I am what I am
Nothing can change that
If you don't like it,
Go fuck yourself
Just don't be a bitch
You want to kill me?
Does your righteous anger impel you to run me over
When I have my face painted and wear flowing clothes
Fuck off
I am
I am and
I am
Love
Love is
And Hate is
What we make them to be
Beautiful or ugly
Your hate is ugly to my eyes
You don't have to kiss me, boy
But you are beautiful to me
I can say that without shame
You are just a fascist cunt
With bullets of unforgiveness and misunderstanding
You can be your ugly self
I can catch my beautiful colors

On a Sony lens
Or around my eyes
Your anger is ugliness all over
You with your cheap despair
    bought with food stamps of indecision
One day love will leave you
Then we will see who's a prisoner
But I am a prisoner for just this long
A prisoner
Of some shallow dream

Ode to the Cerebral King

What intersection are we at,
On our journey toward the stars?
What direction now?
Everything seems to be woven into a multicolored quilt,
	sewn to fit the wearer
We try our best to iron out the wrinkles in our minds,
But those wrinkles are what make thought possible

The songs of the mandolin
And the trips of the travel company
Are all odes to the King
And my words
Spoken down rice fields and acid rain shores
Are all shouts and bows to this cerebral King
Those gallows wait for whosoever may find them
They all serve the King

Sequins drip from the tidal storms of fate
Waiting to be wrapped in clothes of gold
But can I be bestowed with might and majesty
Or is reservation the only rules for splendor
To live in the mind and sparkle on the outside

Attention is granted and words only mean so much
When it is explained to the whirlwinds
        of the flying mannequin dead eyes
There is no life there
When words are gone and wisdom is banished,
Discarded for might of thunder

Save me, O mighty King
From myself
For I know not what I do
Nor how far it will take me
I am carried, breathless,
Forever on the winds of brightness
Take me where I stand
Or leave me where I kneel
At your feet may I rise and gaze upon your envied beauty
Swirl your colors on the canvas of humanity
Can't I share in your grace?
Can I share your flare?
No?
Pine trees stare at the ground but lap up life from the spring
But I leave it to dry beneath Your sky
And I must find a route to reach your Heaven

Triple Trick-or-Treat

Triple Trick-or-Treat happens when a person decides that they want to be something different than what they are. They put on the mask that they want so that the person that is usually not there shines through. But if the mask is on, can anything shine through? Or is it blocked and refracted internally? People must decide what face they want to show to the world and what face they want to show when they are in private. The imagination shows strange things that one might not like about oneself. But we always must see it for what it is and not reject it because the thing about people is that they easily see what they want to see. And what they want to see is not always the truth. Is the truth what comes out when one is not thinking. Is it possible to not think? Things just flow and the flow just comes and the mind stops and the purple fog oozes out of every pore and makes you behave as you would inately behave. Every person has a different nature. We would all react differently to the same situation. But we must tap into what we would initially do and then once we can see it, we can correct it if need be. White and Black doesn't matter. We are all people and we are all inately connected whether we like it or not. We were all created by the same god.

Trampled by the Hands

Tarnished and broken in this unforgiving landscape
Full of undergrown stalagmites,
There is not even a chance that I might reach the ceiling.
I will remain an undergrown
Underprocessed filament
That is only worth being unnoticed
And trampled underfoot by the boots of the socially acceptable.
Everything is black and encrusted with rust that is forever.
Black rust does not ever fall off of my eyes.
My eyes are stapled shut from the ongoing madness
Which is my own scalded life.
Why is time such a cruel taskmaster?
Cracking the whip in the time it takes us to take one step.
It won't even let us get up from our chairs,
Because we know our chairs are already
Dirty with lies
And secrets
And desires.
Oh my God,
Time
Space
And everlasting life

What does the wind foretell in a land without breeze?
Everything is blistering and cracking
          under the foul-smelling lies.
Walking through knee deep sludge
          that forever pulls but never consumes.
I just get deeper and deeper, but I can still breathe
               the polluted air of my dreams,
Forever rotted under the stench of death and destruction,
Time knows but won't tell us
Why we are this way.
Because he created us to suffer.
But in my reality
I can't see anything through these corroded lenses
Except the numbers,
The numbers ticking away my life.
Every second of every hour,
It counts down to my final moment.
So what am I doing with my life?
The final moments come as we are in our darkest hour
But if we are always in our darkest hour,
Consumed by our darkest thoughts,
When is our Time?

Sacred Friend

There is this person...
You may know him
But then again, maybe you don't
For he does not even know himself
His heart and mind are jigsaw puzzles
With pieces hidden in dark unknown places
In far off lands
But I am searching for them
For I am drawn to this person
In ways in which I cannot put into words
I cannot even form abstract thoughts
Full of twists and turns, coming to new walls
And new clues
But I can't get out of this maze
Even if I tried
Because I have fallen
Fallen and magnetized to this person and can't seem
To pull away
Because I don't want to
It's strange,
In this new land of undiscovered secrets,
I am attracted to what I know not

And what I am slowly beginning to know
For the more information I learn,
The more it pulls me in
And the more I feel loved
And the more I feel love
Towards this person.
But in the back of my conflicted mind is the thought
The thought of what is not written
And what is not
And what may not be there
But the hope
And the feeling is what remains
And what drives me forever forward
Toward him.

Reden.
Let's talk
That's what we are here for,
To lean on each other.
Listen,
I hear noises from the darkness,
I cannot make out the sound,
I'm not sure if I should...
Go forward?
Or go two steps back?
Why this battle,
This battle of wits?
Until the ends of the earth in all directions
Time moves and doesn't stop for any of us,
It pushes us on into emotional states,
Where we don't know ourselves

And discover others.
Because,
In discovering others,
We can find ourselves.

Gagged

This world will never be
What I had hoped for
Because every second is like a scalpel
Peeling away at the back of my skull
I can't take much more of the twisted road signs
                    that guide my way
I always thought these demons would keep me company
In my despair
But I found out that the only thing worth fighting for
                    is the darkness
But I already knew that...
But now, everything is escaping from my body
In clouds of phosphorescent smoke
I'm losing everything
And I am breaking into pieces
That cannot be put back together into something
Anything
It is always ugly
Like me
And I can't do anything about it
Because I know deep down that it is what I strive for
And I pull myself back down into the spiral

Because I'm the only one here
The only one in my mind
And infested by the demons of my own making
I ravage myself with knives and guns that I have spawned
From an eternity of torment
Time is not forever in this place
Pain is forever trapped within me
But pain is just weakness leaving the body
With each cut do I get stronger?
I don't feel any different,
I feel smaller
And more distant from everyone and
Everything that I love
I don't want anyone to be hurt by me
So I push them away
To find myself alone
At the bottom
In the dark
Searching for another that is like me...
That maybe can love me...
But I always hurt the ones I care the most about.
I'm like a pill that instead of heals,
Opens the wounds up to be freshly bled out...
I have a one track mind
But that track only leads to death
Or something intricately wrapped in the spirals of loneliness
Please give me a blanket...
Because it's so cold where I am...
I don't know whether time is running out
But the world sure does show that the sun doesn't shine for us
The forgotten ones...
Leaving doesn't seem so strange

In this world of forgotten pleasures
And the only thing we seek is release
I'm too far down now
But the world flourishes
When we die...

A Story

Ripped by barbed wire pulled through each orifice
    of his twisted body,
He hangs above the ocean, begging to be released
    into the depths of nothingness.
He longed for the watery abyss.
It would be the end to all pain, to all of the thorns
    that tear his flesh.
"Pull me down, I say"
He could barely utter these words for barbs
    were tearing his tongue as they ravaged
      up and down his throat.
He couldn't scream.
He couldn't hear, but he could feel
    his nonexistent scream pounding in his head.
His arms were splayed out as blood dripped down his sides,
There was nothing he could do except hang
    and pray for it all to end.

His toes slowly touched the water,
It was cool and refreshing.
And for a moment he forgot all his pain...
But it didn't matter because the flying Shrieks

had decided to take his eyes.
And as his sockets bled nothing except lies and deceit
He cried
Without tears.
For everything he had lost
And everything he had broken.
He wished that the trees would sprout life on his grave.
But everything dies around him,
Because he kills
And maims
And despises.
What does he see?
He stares out across the ocean
        but nothing reaches his empty eye sockets
Because his head is empty
The Shrieks have taken lodging inside his mind
        and won't let him free.
All he can do is tremor because all he knows
        is the seizures that rip his body apart
Because he created this shit.
He produced everything from the dark abyss of his unconscious.
And he accepted it
And embraced it.
Because that was what he was.
And his final thought before he was ripped in two
        and blood poured into the black ocean

was...

Let me into the clouds...

Pull Out the Knife

Everything is tragically overplayed. cut broken discharged onto a canvas that rejects it. Nothing helps because everything is tided down to the cracked table that only cuts into the back of the victim. Jagged jagged and broken until day breaks the clouds and sheds light down on everything. but where has the light gone? I can't fucking find the light, everything is cloaked in darkness and I can't find my way out. help. I fucked up everything. I can't get rid of anything because pain is endless. I can't think because the demons won't leave me alone. I am damaged and violated and tossed aside by everything that was supposed to love me. Why bother? I'm not fucking worth it. I just deserve to be used, fucked and tossed in the gutter. please. Time has no meaning for me, I have been locked, trapped in that time, back then. In that place.. when I was filled... when I liked it... when I didn't know... i feel so small so helpless why what where when how did this happen. Why do I like it. why do I hate it? why must it always happen this way in tiimes of now and longing and pain and despair when disjointed functions enter into me bleeding and dying and penetrating me till I cry out for it to stop....

Please take me as I am

Bleeding

And as a child

taken from behind and penetrated, give it all to me

I

want

it

now

fuck me

cum in me

and make me bleed

I cannot take what is mine because nothing is mine. I am yours forever. You've had me, you broke me, you need me. But I can't find you. Are you still there? in my thoughts...
In me?

I can't feel you. I can't not now. It hurts. Don't make me bleed. Oh got the cum pain callous neither fall nor now nor anything that has come to pass in this lifetime I. I what now. These things I can't control with the now is entering into the past present and future which is the past because I'm stuck.

Always stuck.

I cannot free into the nothingness. penis entrapment. Crammed into a tiny space where I deserve to be, in a treehouse. covered in blood. Why didn't I cry. It's not your fault. things happy. A big star nebular will crack and fall to earth but it doesn't stop. A shot, a petal, a rose, a gun. a drop of blood in the back seat of a car inthralled and entertained with murder. With rape. With all the things that should be withdrawn. Pull out please, I can't take it. It's too big, it hurts.

I can't really think, thoughts don't come naturally. Words do, but not thoughts. I just type and display and feel it drip down the inside of my leg. you've cum, now leave me here. I'm not worth anything, just use me. That's what I'm here for, for your pleasure, I don't need anything anyone. i'm just alone as I cry. It slices into me like a scalpel into a body. Because I"m already dead inside.

Nothing

        ever

happens

              here

I'm dying, suffocating as your penis enters my mouth. But the sexual invades my brain because it's split my hemispheres down the middle and my brain no longer functions normally. I can't really be a normal person, I am evil. bound, broken, gagged, bound, dripping, living, dying, breathing, suffocating, endlessly below the ocean. I am drowning and can't get out. Kill me please. i can't go on.

Pull

out

the

knife...

Ugly

I am the grapes at the supermarket
That people steal as they browse the produce.
Everyone can have a piece of me,
I'm free...
But please know,
That the razor cuts are of my own design
Cut into my arm is what I am
How I look
Who I am
I am
Ugly.
Everybody knows it, though some deny it.
I was put on this earth to bleed completely out
Until nothing is left of me.
I've given myself away throughout the years...
Where's the piece for me?
I can't really find it...
I am tied down to this bed of nails
I slowly sink down as my flesh tears apart.
But I don't feel it.
I don't care anymore.
The pain has become a lifestyle.

What I need.
All I've known.
So why should I expect any different.
I always want what I cannot have...
Which is proof that I don't deserve it.
Because I'm ugly.
Inside
and
Out.
There is nothing good about me.
I have rotted away
As everyone was eating off of me.
I drag the razor down the middle of my chest
And search for something that beats.
But I can't find it.
As I pull my ribs away one by one
I uncover what is buried inside.
As the hole where my heart used to be comes into view,
Mucus and cum pour out of the cavity.
Everything of depravity of malice of hate
Comes pouring out.
This is everything I'm made of.
Hate, perversion, anger, cruelty, sadism, everything made of bile.
There is nothing beautiful that I can find.
Everything worth disgust and loathing.
I so wish I could leave this world behind because,
With all the pain in the world,
I don't need to add to it.
I'm ugly and worthless,
Can't add to the good,
The disgusting is too great, I get lost in it,

No one ever notices me.
I'm nothing.
I don't need to be forgotten
If nobody knows who I am.
I could just disappear.
Into the night.
Free of everything
Free of myself
Free of the harm I cause
Free of the people who take pieces of me
Free of those who hate me
Free of my hate
Free of my wasted life
Sitting boiling in this pot because I know
That hell follows me where I go.
Spiral longing and interchanged with my madness
Nothing makes sense until I rape everything.
The only thing I am capable of is rape.
I will rape your mind.
I will rape your happiness.
I will rape your feelings.
I will rape you.
So keep your distance.
And maybe
When I leave
Everyone will be happy.

Cosmic Love

I grasp blindly through this dense fog
For some words to express
The way I feel.
My mind seems to be deficient.
But I cannot determine whether it was that way
From the start.
So I sit here,
Trying to put my fingertips on the letters
In which I can tell you
How much you mean to me.
Maybe some day
We can find a way
To break down this Berlin Wall which divides us.
But once those stones fall to the ground,
Shattering like broken glass,
I would be waiting on the other side
Ready to run to you.
And embrace you,
And hold you as you cry.
I wish I could tell you that
The storm which is your life will someday
Be calm.

I wish I could erase your pain,
And protect you from all the people who have
Hurt you.
Used you.
Abused you.
I would brush your hair away from your face
And look into your pretty eyes.
"You're not alone,
You don't have to be frozen anymore."
So many people have broken us,
And taken parts of us that we will never get back.
But together, we can be complete.
Even though shards of ice pierced through my soul,
You melted them with your warmth.
I had been kicked aside and dropped in the dirt.
But you were there, holding out your hand.
So I grabbed your hand,
And we stayed connected.
I wish more than anything
That I could lift the weight off of your shoulders
And help you carry it.
I want to take you far away from the black mist
That has almost swallowed you into
It's stagnant lungs.
Everything in this life could drop away,
Be swallowed into the dust.
And if it closed the gap between us,
That would be all that mattered.
Us standing there.
You looking at me,
And me looking at you.
The rubble and remains under our feet.

Our souls dance and mingle with one another.
And nothing else matters,
Because we've found each other.

PART SIX

Tear Out Your Eyes
And I Shall Give
You Wisdom

WALLS

Trapped in this spiral cage, I see things I wish didn't exist.
But they do because I created them
And wanted them to live in this world.
I stretch my arm through my bars to touch the breathing walls.
They drip with fresh mucus that parts to reveal a doorway
         in the pinstriped wall.
Kiss me forever in this death landscape
      where the only way to be is evil.
I wish my intelligence would grow, but these bars hinder me.
My cage finally opens and I step through the striped door down.
GIVE ME THE MONSTERS

MESH

I stumble blindly down the stairs, but then I realize that the only way to see is to lose the eyes. Then what is real reveals itself independent of what's true. Truth marks time in the unbegotten. Crimson flows through my pours as I see without the senses. I am mentally cremated as I fall and am caressed by the stagnant dolls. Their eyes have been gouged out with a radio dial. Visions of lust in this forever vacuum of cardiac arrest. I am raping your dolls, but they can't see me. Blood cotton does not make me feel loved. I drop the violated plastic and wait to be amused. My fire mistress.

Cut Burns

Mommy, why is it cold?

Cold...

Jagged teeth on the event horizon smirk at what I fail to find.
Smear
Through this swamp of everlasting residue.
This is the place where I belong.
Where it's filthy.
Where the usage is apparent.
My body is the smears.
I have been used.
Yet never cleaned.
Forgotten
In this enclosure where the walls seep the blood
        I have given too often.
Seek me now
In this place.
No one hears me
As the tub swallows me into the abyss.

Death

A release

Stone

Hollow is the sound.
Silent is the space.
Frigid dull steel.
I wish for the sharp of it
So I can tear into my flesh
And forget
How filthy I must be.

Water
Recleansing through the contours of white
Cannot take it away.
Forget
How I took it.
How here
Clean
Dirty
Shine
Grime
I can sense the shit below the surface of the hidden.
The obscure.
The stripes of insanity.

I hang
here
Like a towel from a hook.
Trying to desperately scrub away
        the ugliness

Which is

    myself...

My Train

My writing speaks for itself
But does that mean that it does not come from my own mind?
Is it being fed through me?
Making me a cheap passageway for some twisted spirit?
I stand here with my arms open, begging to be taken away
Away from this place,
Because I can't seem to break through this thin layer of plastic.
It bends and gives but never lets me penetrate
      to the other side of what is known.
So I am forever stuck in this darkness
      awaiting my fate which is now doubted.
Always using the same words to express the same meaning,
But can we still express something once that meaning is lost?
Once we are groping desperately for
      something to put down in words.
I just sit here with nothing
Just blankness
And it hurts.
Questioning my purpose in this ever changing ever becoming
      escapeness of carpeted completeness.
How then shall I complete this?
How shall I end it?

With death,
Or with life?
I have not decided whether I should bring down the fire
      on this domain of mice and coincidences
            on all of unconscious subordination of life
                  and equally proficient decadentness
                        of ageless wisdom.
I just don't know much anymore.
I have lost touch with reality and my characters
      and everything that I have become.
I have changed from randomness
      to sheathing my craft and leaving it for dead.
I must not compromise this in full knowledge of its downfall.
And my downfall.
What if I rise up to rule over this world, this domain,
But what then?
To reign chaos on the stupid sheep of this life?
Or to herd them into the shelter away from the storm?
Still, destiny remains a blur.
Remains a distant.
Remains a fluent.
Remains to be fulfilled in its time,
But in my way.
I know I can breathe through and regain,
Regain all that I have lost and the train of thought
      that exited long ago.
I need to board it again.
Because this seems to be my prerogative.
But the problem is I don't even know what that means anymore.
I can't connect meaning to words anymore.
Everything washes together in an incoherent mass of despotism

and rot and filth and everything that I seem to wallow in.
This is the now,
And this is the place I must do it.
And I can, with one fist at a time.
In one way at a time with twisted anarchy
I will become supreme from everything
I have ever dreamed in my head.
I can become the living.
I am the Now.

Grotesquely Living

I have rediscovered the catalyst for recreational disaster
My clock has become timid in this chance distraction
But I have come to realize the true meaning of powerplay
Because I don't fathom entrapment of the enterprising brain
Because I see these things that many trample underfoot
And bequeath from an innocence of longing for the undeniable
But only grant me the ungrantable tendrils of despair
I long for the bottomless pit where I can understand the destiny
Of all things cherishable
Only see the consuming olympics of the forbearers
They have set up the cards
And we must knock them down with full force
Or we die

Give up the now and look only to what's become of the past
Recast and then dismiss all you have failed
Because the dried up cement of conquest
        is only capable of the one thought
That has closed me into the blood dripping quest
            for post-preposterous
Everything is ludicrous but we eat what the clowns
        from the dog pound give us

We are just the race of subliminal advertisements
        in the college of ignorance
Chain me to the palm tree branches of arctic infatuation
All I see now is what I have been given
I cannot pull from what I know not
Or what I have thought up because I can't give life anymore
I see my dead geese that have rotted
        in the blu-ray box with my own wedding
All of us have become scratched dvds
        that will not play on any political decoder
I skip and crack and cannot sputter back to the chapter I was at
Please buff me out
Buff me out until I am shiny in the space
        where all cycles cease to spin
But now I have come to the end of the circle
And the reasoning repeats itself until the start and the stop
            justify each other
And now, without further ado
I shall destroy the cane that has beaten our backs
        into this hateful digital counter
That has kept track of us since our conception
Monitored in the womb we have no say in how we are born
But I will be born soon from my vaginal prison
Covered in fluvial cords
        that just moo their ignorant contentment
I will not stand for the wires that attach me to the moon
I'll pull down
And lift you up into the rays or countless incarcerations
You can kill me until I have really lived
And then I'll be at peace

Cosplay

I want you to tell me something
But I know you won't
Because the reason does not exist
How come? you ask
I shall tell you, I say
Because we are covered with an ever-expanding blanket
A red blanket that blocks out intraviolet light rays
And we only see the mirror that reflects ourselves back at us
What does that show? you say to me
Us, says I
Very, but it isn't very stimulating. reply the jellyfish
On the contrary it is courtesy of the quackmire overarch
The what?
This is why I want you to tell me something
What should I tell you?
Why we look at ourselves.
Because we
What?
We what?
We make things
I make things happen
Yes, but why do we look at ourselves?

I don't know.
But you just said because we.
Yes.
And?
And what?
I just said.
Said what?
That we look at one another.
No, you said we look at ourselves.
We do.
No we don't.
Don't we?
Not one bit.
How so?
We see our projection reflection.
Huh?
Exactly.
Exactly what?
That's exactly it?
What is?
The mirror that we look through.
Is this going anywhere?
The mirror does, yes.
To where?
Everywhere.
You're vague.
Like the world.
I can see.
No you cannot see.
Fuck you.
You cannot fuck me because I do not exist,
      I live beyond the mirror.

So do I.
No, you do not.
Why?
Because I do not see.
See?
Si.
Oh.
Precisely.
Can you tell me something?
No, why?
Because I don't know anything.
No one does.
But you're not just anyone.
I'm not?
No.
What makes you so sure?
Because you are talking directly to my mind.
But that's just your imagination, I am you.
So I am not a typical human.
You're just an ape.
I know.
No, you do not si.
I can see.
No, you cannot.
Fuck, man, this is getting annoying.
You're doing it to yourself.
How?
Because you are writing this.
Why can't I stop?
Because you're narcissistic
        and you think you are something you are not.
What's that?

You think you're god.
I'm not?
No.
Yes I am.
You may think you are, but you are not.
Then who am I talking to?
Yourself.
Then I am god.
Courtesy.
Courtesy of what?
Delusions.
I am not delusional.
What do I know?
Tell me something.
Tell you what?
Anything.
Ok.
Go ahead then.
Why should I?
Because you're wiser than I.
But where do I live?
In that desert between the Corkosoland and Pastramation.
How did you know?
I know of worlds that are not on this plane.
Very good.
Just tell me something.
You will die.
What?
I told you something.
But I already know that...
I did what you asked.
Fine.

Fine.
Cold bastard.
You're just a bitter cynical unknown.
Not for long.
We'll see.
I just don't want to go to sleep dead.

Poppy Seeds and Jolly Ranchers

I wonder if the child I once was would kick me in the balls,
Tell me to man up,
And to stop being a fag.
But nothing would change.
Since
I would only molest my former self,
Violate him and make him squeal in pain.
Then I'd dump him in a blood-stained treehouse where he can sit
And think of how things used to be.

But that's not how it would happen.

To rape oneself is only to destroy part of you
            that once was innocent.
But you'd have to dig farther and farther back in time
            since what was corrupted
So long ago
Was so young.
I have forgiven nothing
And accepted everything.

I can still feel the vines of pity slowly climb up my leg,
Inching toward sinful desire.
I wish that it would all happen again.
But this time
Lay me under a tree canopying our weathered bodies,
Tell me I'm beautiful,
Then make love to me
If only for a moment in time.
But it wasn't that.
It was like scraping away at a potato that is stubborn to peel,
And it is not tender.
And there is no canopy above us.
No beauty
Just wood.
Bark into the interior of mildew.
And I shake again,
Waiting to take inside the watered down world that is made into
A Time Machine.
And a capsule.

What is forgotten is disregarded as useless.
What remains alive in our minds is what we use to fuel our
Darkest Fantastical Entertainments.
And for now I will remember all of it.
In vivid lights and shadows.
Even though it wasn't beautiful,
It became a part of me.
And I became him, deep within the cave of spray-painted daisies.
And for all I see now I can't determine
        if mind memory plays tricks on the User.
For all it is worth, I will pay with experiences.

Give me more and lay me here,
I will wait
Under the stars for you to take me as your slave.
But love me as you would a child.
I shall be your innocent.

Patches

He had flesh
Hands
A beating heart
And blood coursing through his veins.
Yet he felt as if he were fabricated and
Patched together with bits of undeveloped conclusions.
Sewn together from beliefs that didn't fit,
He ended up just being confused and perceived as confusing.
The boy didn't know if he should tear himself apart again
Then try to build himself better.
For the moment, he liked the way he was.

To tell the truth,
He didn't like the way he liked himself.
Because with everything he said,
The yellow yarn that held him together collected in his mouth.
Every statement he made
    got more of the yarn clogged in his mouth and throat.
He knew that sooner or later
    he wasn't going to be able to speak anymore.
He didn't care as long as he could confuse
    as many other patchwork people along the way.

The little patchwork boy would share
        his mismatched squares with whatever
Little boys and girls would cross his path.
They would ask him why his face was different
        on one side than on the other side.
He would shrug and cover the little boy's or girl's mouth up
        with a checkered cloth strip.
He told them that it was in the way that they saw it.
The patchwork boy did not think
        that his face was different on one side.
Those other little boys and girls
        didn't see the real world as he did.

But as time went on,
The patchwork boy could not say anything
        without getting his yellow yarn
Tangled and knotted and in an irreconcilable bunch.
The other boys and girls stopped listening to him because
All the patchwork boy's knowledge amounted to
        was yarn in his head.
So he headed back home, trying to untie himself.
All he managed to do was to pull a button eye out of his head,
And the other eye made of styrofoam.
But he could still see the world.
It was the same.
The way it was all along.
He just saw it without his eyes,
For then, now, and forever.
And when he replaced the eyes with string,
Nothing could loosen his world.

PART SEVEN

Becoming Everything

Perfect Forever

Fall onto and into me
As my body escapes into whatever is left of my soul.
I have become nothing,
And in the process lost everything.
As I whip tentacles of liquid nitrogen
       in a circle around my consciousness,
I realize what I need is the blankets of whatever came before.
But I've always seemed to lose
       whatever could have been beautiful.
Then I open my eyes onto the landscape of bizarre concordances
       that only record my life
Thus far.
But now I know how it continues.
Because I finally understand how it began.
But for now I am still yours.
Still born and in your arms I wait.
I wait till I can finally show you how I'm becoming everything.
For you and for me I know light and shadow
       can be still as the dawn
As time drips my mind from the land I decided not to visit.
Snap off what hasn't happened yet
And create your own forever.

This is a Warning

This is the way you will die.
This is the way you will die.
This is the way you will die.
Not with a bang, but with a whimper.

You will beg,
And no one will hear you.
You will cry,
And they will turn away.
You will curse,
And they all will throw stones.

In your discarded life you wait.
In your discarded life you dream of martyrdom.
But they do not give you satisfaction
of innocent bystander green radiation of why
      and now as nothingness
why as everythingness and finally you believe in your talentless talent in winged chariots of bliss riding into a blazing horizon for-ever burning madness and hate only for oneself but why in this consummation as I consume the heat of your purity As the purple

I see bleeds forever into my eyes. give me, but I already know I can. And I commence with 7 to continue to completion.

Spindle Trap

Triangulate my throat
And slit a hole so deep that I would
        never be able to climb back out.
Stabbing at the trachea with giant knitting needles,
I slip back into the mucus.
To finally become Seven, I need to reach
        the knowledge suspended in the
                splintered air behind the throat.
Body is a prison for the soul.
We are hollow, trapped, and dead
Inside our blood vessels.
You are a wheel postponed indefinitely
And I am your flat.
Come and fill me to tipping.
But then I fall into the Spindle Trap.
Forever being carried on a cloud of spider tongues.
And forever impaled on woven cotton.
I prick my finger,
It has just begun.
Inject your arm down my oiled throat as I beg you
To save me.
Everything is illuminated

And I asphyxiate on your loveliness.
Seduction isn't what it seems
And premonition may be wrong
But I know for a fact,
Parting ways always leads to strawberry paragons.

Bone Goggles

They come from below my eyes
Trekking through the path of my tears.
I gladly let them infect as their capes of steel
      make incisions in my cornea.
And I focus through my blood,
Seeing only malice and the fire that rapes my severed torso.
My head waits in silence,
In a sand sarcophagus
Until you kiss my exposed spine.
Heal the way my eyes project daggers into your love lips.
Don't say it because the Bone Goggles won't let me believe it.
I only know my pain,
And I only see your death
Through bloody cartilage.
But
      Please
Help
      Me
To discard the ocular falsifiers
And revive my spirit into your arms.

Becoming Everything

Forget forever
And come down to paradise.
Where everything becomes nothing
And the spiral of sheep trace back to the end of
Always beginning.
But I know
That Finding Eden
Will not always wash away
Like waterfalls of forgiveness.
I die anyway in the bright swamp of cowardess.
Forgive me, but not
Knowingness of sky radiance
In your face of unbliss.
I'm here in your fleshless arms
Waiting.

I work better when I'm broken.

waiting
forever forever forever forever forever forever forever
forever forever forever forever forever forever forever
forever forever forever forever forever forever forever

forever forever forever forever forever forever forever
forever forever forever forever forever forever forever
forever forever forever forever forever forever forever
forever forever forever forever forever forever forever

FUCK FOREVER
eternity

In the moment.
Only for now.
Only for this long.
And it is taken from my hands
Into your mouth of defiance,
And I am pushed from everything I desire.
And you refuse to give.
You don't need to give in,
But why refuse to give?

For I love you in this,
And not just for now,
Not just for this moment.
eternity
That's what I wish.
I wish for these things you can't provide.
But take me anyway
As I plummet upwards
Toward non-redemption.

As it is in this it is
And I
And You

And Us
none
no one
In this is blameless.
As I am becoming everything,
You give me nothing
Except an empty embrace.
It's just a continual NO.

It seems, as I instinctively fall into cloudlessness,
That I am slowly beginning to see things
Even though I cannot identify them.
Now and them you are king.
And I know this as a knife entering the air.
As the wind breaks the skin,
I can feel time draw me in as a lover.
But I don't want it to penetrate me
        like a sponge in scalding water.
We are our fears.
And into this world we inject our thoughts,
And reject sensibilities,
As we crave death in hollowness.

It takes strength to give yourself to the world.
And through living it creates incantations of spirit waves
Into the ocean of collective.
Why do I want this more than experience itself?
Eluded delusions become realizations when we make it so.
In dreams we are one.
In dreams I see you.
In dreams we understand one another.
Give to me

As I give to you.
Simultaneously entering each other.
Blue energy canals of radiant spectacles
Circle our entity
In time space.
Free us into the atmosphere
As we make love to all things being.

I know you.
Open your eyes to the breaking outer reaches
As my fingers stretch to touch you.
I'll split off and my body can be in many.
Because it is not me who is becoming everything.
As long as I'm a prisoner in this,
I can't reach out.
But everyone
In everything
We all are

As we spin in space
We merge into Light
And Dark
And Good
And Evil
And Everything
And Nothing
We are Together
We are You
We are Us
We are Everything

Finding Eden

I have forgotten how to dream
I have forgotten how to cry

However, this is my world, Forever
I have created it
And I can destroy it.
I have discovered
And I have lost.
Without Forever is something I will have to live in.
Eden has brought me into the lush landscape
Then spit me out like a fish without it's bones.

You are Still and Perfect
You are Still and Forever
But I know now that underneath everything in the dirt
Is the Sun.
And beneath every dead shell is a spirit,
Wafting somewhere on the breeze as one consciousness.
And I still have to find it.
Always Chasing Amy.
It wasn't all in vain,
All withered like a weed without a gardener.

It wasn't all useless,
As I am laying here in invisible arms.

Touchness

Touchless

Toothless and decaying in the Garden
        of Eden.
You are beautiful,
Not forever on this Earth,
But forever inside me.
Teach me your sins so that I can make them my own.

I shall walk,
        In the Shadow,
In the Light of Inspiration Knowing.
You have dragged me here,
Kicking,
        Screaming,
                Hiding my Face,
Then Accepting.

Timecode my life.
Do I start at Zero or at One?
Eden is like a sky captured in time-lapse:
Wispy, white perfection slipping away on a blue darkening.
How did I find it in this wasteland
        of ever-present float nothingness?
I did,
No Timecode inside that spectrum of solace.
No Burn-In with me without a shadow of space.

I did not have a Screener to show me
        how this was going to turn out.

That is life,
Without metaphor, without fancy meaningless words.
Life.

To live in the present,
To aspire for the sky and the blue darkening
        into something amazing,
is Enough for me.
I'll gladly look for Eden for the rest of my life.

What shape do you hold?

Seven

I am the daughter of Finality.
The sister of Apocalypse.
The wife of Extinction.
The priestess of Rape.
The mother of Despair.
And the seductress of Deception.

There seem to be no buttons to control this life.
So I've taken it upon myself to manipulate the spirit.
And I understand now what it means
      to hope for the desperation.
I have followed my path toward divinity,
And discovered femininity, and absent virginity.
Speak to me in hushed whispers as you create the substance.
This substance of emptiness in Tantra.
I live by nothingness,
And my only god is Zero.
Emptiness is an easy concept,
Infinity flushes away our consciousness and leaves us
In a flooded desert drowning in our ignorance.
I am here to put out the fire with flames.
I am here to warm the cold women with ice.

And if you bother to love me,
I'll share with you what has become single
       inside our constellations.
How we find hope.

The box that I keep under my bed is filled with chipped teeth,
Neglected by the tooth fairy of my desires.
I covet her dress and her powers,
And what she stirs up in the young.
If there is a way to undress the lies,
What then will we find to put behind bars?
My conscience goes backwards.
My desire is to unmake,
But in hopes of rebuilding.
There is still beauty in the dilapidated,
So why aren't we happy with the rubble we are scattered in?
And the pain we feel is only a temporary pleasure,
Holding on to it is an art that is learned.

Scars given to butterflies
Lie down in daffodils of blood.
As we smell the perfume of factories,
We strip paintings of gravel ceilings holding up our hands
Into the dry air as we crack, crumble, and embrace our lungs.
I haven't got time to grow another pair of hands,
And I certainly can cremate with my own two feet.
Paint me up, make me certain, then I'll be free.

I haven't even begun,
But this is your finale.
My overture will start momentarily.

But for now,
Wait for me, my darlings.
You won't live for much longer.

I SEAL THIS WITH A KISS

In filmic terms, I am dead. As my creativity dies, my skills have curdled. Reels of celluloid wrapped around my neck. It cuts into my trachea. The blood that seeps into the film creates pictures. These are my films. I bleed them and ejaculate them onto my subconscious scrotum, cut open and balls hanging limp in the hands of my invisible mistress. She has my neck, my wrists, my ankles, my anus. They are hers to possess, cut, and reject. Possess me, Forever, but nothing lasts, Forever. I will serve as long as I can. This business has collared me. The art has me in its competitive claws. The hooks are in my spinal column as I am spread eagle naked on your water bed of broken glass.

As long as I cum blood,
I will love you sweetly.

With a gun.

ALL MY LOVE,

7

forever intricate it hasn't happened yet and
forever. I dunno why I'm writing this, but I feel that
something has to be said in the now and you're not
awake to the traverse incantation force ification. I
love you and i don't understand why you can't say
it unless you don't feel the same way for me.
Disregard this message because it means nothing in
space when everything is happening
for a reason and you are the perfect forever
in my arms and I know that
everything happens into itself and
the world makes it so. Just know I
love you and I know you don't
understand but it's the same when
falling apart is perfect and lovely.
Why must you be so cold. This is
beautiful in you. You are beautiful
and I am seven. I need your love to
make me complete and I'm still at a
loss as to how you really feel. I love
you. I really do. But if you don't feel
the same way I need to know. And
disregard this in eternity, I don't know forever as
you. Whimsical spirits speak to my being as your
thoughts flutter in my mind always. I need you.
But I will talk to you tomorrow probably and
negate everything I say here, but know I love you
for always even though you may not. You are the

Love a constant shifting dream. A fleeting moment that feels like forever but never is. You are a moment i am trying to regain. Like a snapshot of a lover you cant seem to find space for in your room. I cant bring myself to utter words of eternal love when in till i know your place

in my heart

You say i am forever, then give me my forever to find the 7.

Forever can be fleeting.

Don't negate what you really mean to say.

-forever

PERFECT
FOREVER

Avtar Simrit is a modern mystic and an artist. His writings and art are inspired by mystical inquiry as well as all inner and outer journeys. Avtar's main artistic mediums are the written word, Hip Hop music, and video. To check out his music and other work, visit the author's website: www.mc-pan.com.

ABOUT THE AUTHOR (from 2011)

Avtar exists in the world, and therefore it is his duty to explore it. One way he does that is through writing. He twirls intricate patterns with images through esoteric wordplay and eccentric metaphors. Other than writing, his interests lie in experimental filmmaking. He is always pushing the boundaries of consciousness through many different art forms. Avtar's long term aspirations include writing and directing feature films, writing books, performing music, and eventually owning his own production company, publishing company, record label, and/or all of the above.